All About

Eeyore

This book belongs to . . .

Meet Eeyore

If we were to tell Eeyore that you were here to meet him, he would probably nod gloomily and say, "Really? I'm sure it can't be me you're looking for . . . there must be some mistake." Eeyore is, after all,

a far-from-merry soul.

You can usually find him standing in a patch of prickly thistles, gazing sadly at the ground, wondering to himself. But all his friends in the Hundred Acre Wood love him very much, and even if he isn't always very good Company, Eeyore appreciates any kindness or friendship that happens to come his way.

In which we read about

Eeyore

It was very cold in the Hundred Acre Wood, for it had been

snowing

and

snowing

and

snowing.

It had been snowing so much that Eeyore, who usually lived in Eeyore's Gloomy Place by the stream (so as not to bother anybody), had decided that it was time he had somewhere warmer to live.

So he had slowly
and gloomily
collected some
sticks and then
placed them sadly in
a pile that looked a bit like a house. After that,
he had gone for a melancholy wander to think about
the state of things in the Hundred Acre Wood.

Later that day,
he returned to
where he had
built his house of
sticks to find that
it wasn't there. Miserable and befuddled,
he ambled to Christopher Robin's house.

"Hello, Eeyore!" said Christopher Robin cheerfully when he opened the door.

"It's snowing still," observed Eeyore, gloomily. "And f r e e z i n g cold. And I don't suppose you've seen a house or what-not anywhere about?"

"What sort of a house would that be, Eeyore?"

"My house. At least I thought it was my house as I built it. But the strange thing is, it was there when I left it this morning and when I came back it wasn't. Not at all natural."

"Oh Eeyore, that's terrible," said Christopher Robin. "We must go and look for it at once." And he went to fetch his coat straight away.

Christopher Robin and Eeyore set off together with Eeyore mumbling about how he couldn't really expect to have a house and he wasn't complaining, but it really wasn't what one could call

Hot at 3 o'clock in the morning these days . . .

Soon they arrived at the corner of the field where Eeyore's house was no longer.

At least there's some snow left," muttered Eeyore. "I suppose I shouldn't complain."

And at that moment, Christopher Robin hushed him and told him to listen.

In the distance they could hear a deep gruff voice singing about the snow and a small high voice tiddely-pomming in between.

"It's Pooh and Piglet!" said Christopher Robin excitedly.

"Quite possibly," replied Eeyore.

And then the words of the song changed and they heard, *"We've finished our HOUSE!"* followed by *"It's a beautiful HOUSE!"* (with *Tiddely-pom* in between).

"Pooh!" called Christopher Robin and the singing stopped.

"It's Christopher Robin!" they heard Piglet say. "He's round by the place where we got all those sticks from."

The friends rushed to meet each other and when
they had hugged hello, Christopher Robin began
to explain the sad story of Eeyore's Lost House.
As Pooh and Piglet listened, their eyes got

bigger

and

bigger.

"*Where* did you say it was?" asked Pooh.

"Just here," replied Eeyore. "Made of sticks."

"Oh," said Piglet rather nervously, and began to

hum *tiddely-pom* so as to appear quite at ease.

"What's the matter?" said Christopher Robin.

"Well," began Pooh. "The fact *is*," said Pooh. "The fact is, you see . . ." said Pooh. "Well, we thought it might be warmer at the other side of the wood."

"Warmer for what?" asked Christopher Robin.

"For Eeyore's house," said Pooh firmly.

Eeyore tried to say that his house had been *here*, but before he could mumble very much, Pooh and Piglet had led him round the corner. And there was Eeyore's house, looking as comfy as anything.

"It has an Inside as well as an Outside,"
explained Pooh proudly.

And just to make sure, Eeyore went inside . . .
and came out again.

"Quite remarkable," he said at last. "The wind must
have blown it here. And somehowit got better on the way."

"Much better,"

said Pooh and Piglet together.

And with that, leaving Eeyore in his house,

Pooh and Piglet took Christopher Robin

back for lunch and, on the way, told him of the

Awful Mistake they had made.

Luckily, Christopher Robin laughed a lot.

A few weeks later, when the snow had disappeared
and he was well and truly settled in his new house,
Eeyore was plodding slowly down the stream when
Winnie-the-Pooh appeared.

"Good morning, Eeyore!"

said Pooh, cheerfully.

"Good morning, Pooh Bear," replied Eeyore gloomily. "If it is a good morning," he added.

"Oh dear, what's the matter?" said Pooh.

Eeyore explained that there was nothing, **absolutely nothing,** not even a tiny thing the matter, and that he really wasn't complaining, for it couldn't matter less, and that he really shouldn't be sad on his birthday which, after all, was the happiest day of the year . . .

"Your *birthday?*" said Pooh in surprise.

Eeyore said that of course it was his birthday and couldn't Pooh see all the presents lying around and the birthday cake with candles and pink icing?

Pooh was rather puzzled, for he couldn't see any presents at all. Or, for that matter, any cake with candles and pink icing.

"I can't see any of those things," he said.

And Eeyore grunted miserably and agreed he couldn't see them either, ha ha.

Pooh scratched his head and wished Eeyore many happy returns of the day anyway.

Then, leaving Eeyore to mutter
about nobody taking any notice of his birthday,
Pooh hurried home as quickly as he could.
He felt very sad about Eeyore
and wanted to find him a present.

Outside Pooh's house,
Piglet was jumping

up

and

down,

trying to reach
the knocker.

"Hello, Pooh!" said Piglet.

"I was just coming to see you . . ."

"I've just seen Eeyore," interrupted Pooh.
"And he's in a Very Sad Condition because it's
his birthday and nobody has taken any notice.
He's very Gloomy indeed.

We must take him a present."

The two friends went inside Pooh's house and Pooh went straight to his honey cupboard to see what he could find. He had lots of honey pots but only one with any honey left inside!

"I'm going to give this to Eeyore," he said proudly.

Piglet thought for a moment and then he remembered that he had one balloon left from his party and would go and get it to cheer up Eeyore.

And so Pooh set off with his jar of honey and Piglet
trotted home to fetch the balloon.

It was a warm day, and Pooh began to get
a *funny* feeling creeping over him, from
the tip of his nose, right down to the end
of his toes.

He knew that feeling. It was a feeling that told him
that it was time for a **little something**.

And, with that, he sat down and took the lid off
his jar of honey.

He began to eat,

and eat . . .

and

eat

And as he licked the last drop of honey, he
wondered where it was he had been going.

"Ah, yes, Eeyore!" he said. And then "Bother!"
when he realised he'd eaten Eeyore's birthday
present. *What could he give him instead?* He
thought for a while and then decided that the pot
was a very nice pot even without the honey inside,
and surely Eeyore might find it Useful.

Pooh continued on his way, and as he was passing Owl's house in the Wood he called in to see him. Showing Owl his Useful Pot for Eeyore, Owl said that he should write *"A Happy Birthday"* on it. Pooh thought that was a very good idea and asked Owl to help him.

Which he did, nodding wisely as he wrote:
HIPY PAPY BTHUTHDTH THUTHDA BTHUTHDY.
("A Very Happy Birthday with love from Pooh.")

Meanwhile, Piglet had
fetched his balloon and was
holding on to it very **tightly**
so that it wouldn't blow away.
He *ran* as fast as he could,
so that he might get to Eeyore before Pooh, and
thinking just how pleased Eeyore was going to be,
he forgot to look where he was going.

His foot landed in a rabbit hole and he fell
flat on his face:

BANG!!!!

For a moment, Piglet wondered what

could have happened.

Had the Forest fallen down?

Or had he blown up?

Perhaps he was far away on the moon . . . then he looked

down and realised that it was *he* who had fallen down and

that his poor balloon had popped and

was now nothing more than

a small piece of rag.

"Oh dear!" said Piglet.

"Oh dear, oh dear,

oh dearie dearie dear."

Now his present for Eeyore wasn't such a good one.

Never mind, perhaps Eeyore didn't like balloons so very

much anyway? He would still take it to him, so he trotted

on sadly to the stream where Eeyore was.

Eeyore was just gazing at his reflection in the water, concluding that it was a very sorry sight, when he heard Piglet's voice behind him.

"Good morning, Eeyore!" said Piglet. "And many happy returns of the day!"

Eeyore turned around gloomily and stared at Piglet.

"I've brought you a present!" continued Piglet, excitedly. "It's a balloon!"

Eeyore could feel his gloom slipping away. Now he was getting a balloon it really did feel like a birthday.

"But Eeyore," continued Piglet.

"I'm *SO* sorry,

SO very,

very sorry,

I'm afraid when I was bringing it to you I fell

over and I

BURST

the balloon."

There was a long silence.

"*My* balloon?" said Eeyore
at last, and Piglet nodded. He held
out the little piece of damp rag.
Eeyore looked at it and Piglet felt
really rather miserable.

But Eeyore didn't seem too upset and asked Piglet what colour it had been when it was a balloon. When Piglet told him that it had been red, Eeyore said, "Thank you, Piglet. My *favourite* colour."

Just then, Winnie-the-Pooh arrived.

"Happy Birthday, Eeyore!" he called.

"I've brought you a present too."

He gave Eeyore the Useful Pot and Eeyore became quite excited.

"Look, little Piglet!" Eeyore exclaimed.

"I do believe that the balloon you gave me will fit very nicely into this rather Useful pot!"

Piglet looked on hopefully as Eeyore
put the balloon in the pot.

"There you are!" said Eeyore.

And Pooh and Piglet were very happy indeed
that Eeyore was so pleased with his presents.

In fact, when it came to say

goodbye

and

Happy Birthday

once again, Eeyore hardly
noticed that his friends were going, for he was
far too busy taking the balloon

out and

putting it back in again,

happy as can be.

What a perfect present!